Onyx Kids

School Days

Book Six

The Spooky Cipher

By Rita Onyx

Onyx Star Publishing, LLC
Delaware, USA

Table of Contents

Chapter 1

Wicked Wakeup Prank

The door slowly creaked open and then there was silence. A moment later, soft footsteps, muffled from socks, inched ever so gently to the target.

Silence again. The intruder leaned over the bed and stood there–silently. The intruder and the target were face to face now, although the target didn't know that yet.

"WAKE UP!"

Shiloh's eyes flew open and right in front of his face was a creepy clown mask.

"AAAAHHH!!" He yelled, as he rolled sideways and hit the floor with a loud thump.

He tried desperately to crawl away, but his leg was caught by the intruder's grasp. He yanked his leg hard which threw him sideways landing him on his back. He was about to scream again but got a better look at his attacker. Shasha!

Shasha peeled the mask off and was crying with laughter. "I can't believe you fell for that! Ow! My side hurts from laughing so hard!"

Shiloh, exhausted from the whole episode, laid on the floor to catch his breath. "I can't believe you did that to me! You know, I wouldn't do that to you. I wouldn't wake you up from your sleep and scare the–

He stopped midsentence.
He couldn't believe what she
was doing next.

"And that's how you wake up
your brother for Halloween
week. See you guys later!"
Shasha spoke to her phone.

"You are not posting this," he
demanded.

"Of course, I am. That's the
whole point. I can't just tell
my followers what
happened. They need to see
it. Trust me, it was funny,
and you'll go viral." Her
fingers flew over her phone
as she edited and uploaded
it.

"Shasha! Don't post it!" He
tried to get to her in order to
yank the phone out of her
hand, but she was too fast
for him. She jumped over

him and before he could turn around she was already out the door.

"Shiloh, are you awake? Come and eat breakfast. Let's go, let's go! You don't want to be late," His mom called from downstairs.

"Coming!" Shiloh shook his head. *I can't believe Shasha did that. I'm going to get her back. I don't know how, but I will. This week. She can count on that.*

***

As Shiloh walked downstairs he heard his mom roaring with laughter. *I wonder what's so funny.*

Oh.

His mom was looking at Shasha's phone. *So that's what's so funny.*

"I hope you know that I was sound asleep, and it was terrifying to wake up to that clown mask. I'd like to see how you all would react if that were you."

His mom tried to wipe the smile from her face and stifle her laughter, but there was no hope. She let it all out again and was howling.

"It's not that funny," he remarked.

"Actually, it is," Shiloh's mom pointed at the screen. "Your face…"

"I know. I was there," Shiloh pouted as he sat down to eat his oatmeal and fruit. He heard his dad whistling as he walked in from the hallway. "When dad sees this, he'll take my side and he won't think it's funny."

"I won't think what's funny?" his dad asked.

"Hon, look at this," his mom took Shasha's phone and played the video of the rude awakening.

Shiloh watched intently as his dad at first raised his eyebrows, then purse his lips, and finally cover his mouth with his hand. He tried to cover his laugh with a clear of the throat, but it was no use. He busted out laughing too.

"Not you too Dad!" Shiloh
pleaded.

"I'm sorry…" He couldn't
even finish his sentence
because he was laughing so
hard.

"And that's my parent's
reacting to my earlier video
of me pranking my brother,"
Shasha said into her phone.

"Now you're filming
reactions?" Shiloh asked
incredulously.

"I have to juice this. Good job little bro. Until next time," She said as she grabbed her lunch bag and headed out.

"You're right. Until next time. That's a promise," Shiloh said smugly.

"What's that supposed to mean?" Shasha stopped in her tracks.

"Two can play this game. Trust me. I'll have my own viral video. And soon," Shiloh said knowingly.

"Mom, Dad, Shiloh is…" She didn't know what to say.

Shiloh turned back to his parents who were watching their exchange. "It's only fair. But don't go too far you two," his mom said. She shrugged and turned back to cooking.

All Shiloh did was smile at his sister. He started to laugh creepily and bugged out his eyes.

"Don't do that. You look creepy," Shasha said and stalked out.

He kept on laughing until he turned and saw his parents giving him a weird look. He stopped and cleared his throat and grabbed his lunch too.

"See ya later, I'm going to walk to school today." He hurriedly ran out and tried to catch up with his sister. Maybe he could prank her on the way to school.

***

Unfortunately for him, he couldn't catch up to her even though he tried his hardest. *She must have ran the whole way.*

When he got to the parking lot he saw her slip inside the school entrance. She peeked her head out and saw him from a far and stuck her tongue out before she went back in.

Shiloh stepped inside the building and scanned the hallway looking for his best friend Evan. He didn't see him, so he decided to text him:

Hey, are you here yet? I'm right in front of Ms. Suffering's classroom.

In a flash, Evan wrote back:

I'll be right there. I was down in my lab.

Lately, Evan had been down in the lab early in the mornings. He wondered what Evan was planning because he knew that the more time Evan spent down in the lab, the more likely there was some big project he was working on.

"Shiloh," a sharp voice called.

"Oh no," Shiloh muttered. He slowly turned around at the harsh annoyed voice.

Ms. Sufferin was right behind him scowling at him. She was in her usual old-fashioned gray dress and what she called her "sturdy" shoes, which really meant ugly. She saw him look her outfit over and scowled even deeper.

"Why don't you take a picture, it'll last longer," she smirked as she patted her stiff hair.

Ew! Did she really think that he was checking her out?! That was the grossest thing he could've ever thought, EVER. He quickly averted his eyes.

Just then, Evan ran up. "Shiloh, you're not going to believe this!" He was so excited that he didn't see Ms. Sufferin standing right behind Shiloh.

"Believe what?" Ms. Sufferin asked.

"Uh...nothing," Evan said sheepishly. He didn't want to

tell his secret to a teacher, especially *this* teacher.

"You seemed like it was something a minute ago. Why don't you tell us what we're not going to believe. Go ahead young man."

Evan looked at Shiloh for help. All Shiloh could do was shrug. There was no help once you were in the crosshairs of Ms. Sufferin.

"You're not going to believe...how big of a dump–

"WHAT?! I do not want to hear that Evan. That is disgusting. You know what I can't believe? I can't believe that I have such monstrous students in my class. This is absolutely horrifying." Ms. Sufferin stormed off. Before she made it into her class, she turned around and gave them a piercing stare.

"Shiloh, don't be late," she said icily.

Shiloh started laughing so hard. "You are savage. I would've never thought about saying that in front of her. You got rid of her real quick."

"I don't know why she got so upset. I really did see a huge dump truck today. I think it was transporting something." Evan looked confused.

"Ooohh, you mean you didn't...never mind. What were you really going to say?" Shiloh asked.

"Oh yeah...my lab is haunted."

Chapter 2

Charlie Cheese and Pumpkin Pizza

"Haunted! What do you mean your lab is haunted?" Shiloh asked skeptically.

"I mean my lab is haunted," Evan stated matter-of-factly.

"What? How—

"Someone found my lab and left a creepy jack-o-lantern with a strange message carved in it," Evan explained.

"That is so weird! I wanna see it." Shiloh started as if he was going to go to the lab.

"Wait, after we go to homeroom maybe we can run down there. It won't help if we're late and Mr. Thomas and Ms. Suffering are down our backs."

"Mr. Thomas down your back? I don't think so. He's the nicest teacher here. Now Ms. Suffering..." Shiloh rolled his eyes.

"Ok, we'll meet in the lab after homeroom. See you then." Evan ran off.

Shiloh turned to go into his homeroom too. As he made his way to his desk he noticed Ms. Suffering's narrowed eyes trained on him, waiting for him to make a mistake so she could yell at him again.

"Hi Shiloh," His friend Desirae waved at him.

"Hey–

"No talking! Find your seats students," Ms. Suffering ordered.

Shiloh turned around to find Ms. Suffering with a smirk on her face. She looked happy that she found some way to correct him. He made his way to his seat and sat down.

Desirae mimed sorry to him.

Shiloh shrugged and nodded his head to let her know that it was fine.

"Alright class, as we head into the holiday season, we are going to learn about a few things. What kind of holiday would it be if we didn't learn something?"

Someone murmured, "A fun one." The class erupted in giggles.

"Quiet! Who said that?" Ms. Suffering immediately looked at Shiloh.

"I didn't say anything!" he exclaimed.

"Are you shouting at me?"

"No, I uh, I meant. I didn't say anything ma'am." Shiloh looked at his Apple watch to see how many more minutes he would have to endure of this torture.

"Well, I don't care who said it. Not another word from anyone until I'm done." She looked around with her sternest look to emphasize her point.

"As I was saying, the holiday season is upon us which means, everything is about to be tainted with pumpkins.

Pumpkin spice, pumpkin pie, pumpkin bread, pumpkin muffins, pumpkin ice cream, even pumpkin *Pop tarts*, which I just don't understand." She made a gagging noise.

"To add to the horror, we're going to have a contest on the best pumpkin recipe."

The class started buzzing with excitement.

"The rules are that it has to be unique. It can't be something sold in the grocery store already."

"This is going to be really hard!" Roxy, another one of Shiloh's friends said.

"Yes Roxy, it is. I want to see how creative you all can be. Mr. Thomas' homeroom class will also be participating. To make it fair, the items will be set on the tables anonymously and we'll taste them and vote on the one that is the tastiest, if it's possible. You see class, I think injecting pumpkin into everything is horrible but clearly, I may be in the minority since the whole world explodes into pumpkin spice every year. I'm on a mission to see if my mind and taste buds can be changed. Can I enjoy pumpkin flavored food? That is the question. To start, we're going to take a field trip to a pumpkin patch."

The class was already excited but now they erupted in joy that they were going to go on a field trip.

Shiloh texted Evan:

Did you hear that we're going on a field trip?

Evan texted him back:

Yeah, I just heard. What do you want to make out of pumpkins? I'm thinking Pumpkin Pizza.

Shiloh texted Evan:

Pumpkin Pizza! That's disgusting!

Evan texted him back:

Gotta go...Mr. Thomas is staring at me while I'm texting.

"Settle down class! I guess you don't care about the prize. Maybe Mr. Thomas' class does...maybe I'll just go over there and announce it."

There was silence immediately.

"Ok, there will be three prizes. First, second and third. The third prize will be a $20 gift card for Charlie Cheese Pizza."

Another student interrupted, "Isn't that a low-budget knock off of–

"Quiet! I happen to like their pizza. It reminds me of my dear old mother...when she used to make me order pizza because she didn't want to cook." The class snickered.

"Second place gets a thousand...let me see...what is this? V-Bucks? What are V-Bucks?" Ms. Suffering paused for a second and adjusted her glasses as she read her paper.

The class was delirious with excitement.

"Oh, my mistake, I think I need new glasses. C-Bucks, you get a thousand C-Bucks which you can use on the new Charlie Cheese Pizza online computer game."

The class groaned.

"What's wrong? I'm sure it will be just as fun as any of the other games you all play." She shook her head. "Kids these days," She muttered.

"Now for first place. This is really special."

"Let me guess, a Charlie Cheese phone that probably

only dials their number," Max said.

Max was sort of a friend of Shiloh's but lately he hadn't seen him around. Shiloh thought maybe Max was upset because he, Evan, and Desirae had left him out of their projects and other stuff. He wasn't a bully, but he could be blunt and intimidating if you didn't know him.

"How did you know?" Ms. Suffering gave him a shocked look.

"WHAT! I was joking around." Max started crying with laughter.

"Yes, class you get your very own C-Phone. Doesn't it look nice?" She held up a plastic looking blue and yellow phone. "Now you can order your very own Charlie Cheese Pizzas whenever you want."

Shiloh was done with the whole contest. There was no way he wanted to win any of these prizes. They were all trash!

It was as if Ms. Suffering could read everyone's mind. "They're donating a new computer for our computer lab, so we have to do this contest. So, if you don't participate you get an F."

"Is it as ugly as the phone?" Someone asked.

"You mean, is it as unique? Yes. Aren't you all tired of black, gray, or silver? These slick smooth futuristic

designs are so plain. We
need color in our life!"

"Says the lady who dresses
in gray every day." Shiloh
whispered. He thought this
whole thing was so weird.

"I heard that. I want
everyone on their best
behavior because waiting in
the hallway to give you a
taste of their new fall
flavored pizza is Charlie
Cheese! Come on in
Charlie!"

A huge rat mascot wearing a
blue and white shirt and blue
and white sneakers jumped
into the classroom, followed
by a couple of miserable
looking teenagers carrying a
several boxes of pizza.

"Hey class! Charlie Cheese
here!" He did a little dance
that reminded Shiloh of
something he's seen his
parents do.

"Welcome Charlie. We are
so excited to have you here,"
Ms. Suffering gave the class
a threatening look.

Everyone perked up right
away and plastered on
smiles.

"Ew! A giant rat!" Roxy
screamed.

"No, not a rat. That's the other guys. I'm a giant mouse," Charlie corrected her. "Big difference."

"Anyways, check out our new fall-inspired pizzas. We have pumpkin pizza, with turkey sausage. Over there is cranberry cheese pizza with stuffing-stuffed crust. That's right, stuffing is in the crust. Yum! Lastly, we have caramel apple pizza for dessert. Enjoy!" The workers opened the pizza one by one with smiles that looked just as fake as the class's smiles.

Shiloh was underwhelmed at this. He wondered why they couldn't have regular pizza like normal people.

"We'll save the pizza for lunch. Let's give Charlie and

his friends a hand." Ms.
Suffering started clapping.
Two other people joined in
half-heartedly. She scowled
at the rest of the class.

"You can go next door to Mr.
Thomas's classroom where
he's expecting you. Thank
you." Ms. Suffering ushered
them out.

Shiloh quickly texted Evan:

Someone stole your idea.
Get ready for the grossest
lunch you'll ever eat.

Evan texted back:

What are you talking
about?

Shiloh responded:

You'll see.

Desirae raised her hand to say something. "I don't understand. I thought you were on a mission to see if you would like pumpkin flavors."

"I am. My mission is being sponsored by Charlie Cheese Pizza. Look, we need a new computer and they just so happen to be celebrating their three-month anniversary."

"They've only been open three months?" Max asked incredulously, "At this rate, with flavors like those, they'll be closed in a week."

"I can't believe they stayed open three days, much less three months," someone else interjected.

Ms. Suffering folded her hands and gave the class her meanest look. "Like I said before, you must participate. If you don't, then you get an F for the project. So let's see some smiles and let's eat some pizza!"

Just then, the bell rang, causing a stampede to get out of the classroom and away from Ms. Suffering and her icky pizza.

Chapter 3

Don't All Girls

Shiloh ran out of homeroom and almost right into Evan who had raced out of his classroom too.

"I think I lost my appetite for lunch and the day barely started," Evan complained.

"Let's go down to the lab now. I want to see if it's haunted like you claim it is," Shiloh said sarcastically.

"Seriously Shiloh, no one knows about the lab except for us and Desirae."

"Don't forget about Roxy. She knows too."

"Yeah, but she was sworn to secrecy. She doesn't seem

like the type to go around gossiping."

"Don't all girls do that though? Shiloh asked.

"Don't all girls do what?" Desirae came up behind them as they were talking.

"Umm...nothing," Shiloh stammered. He was caught off guard.

"Evan?" Desirae turned to him to see if he would answer.

"You look pretty," Evan said to distract her and because he really did think so. Evan had a crush on Desirae for a long time, but it wasn't going anywhere. He decided to try a new tactic by doing the opposite of what he was

doing. Mainly, he decided to
be more confident.

"Thanks Evan, but if you
think that by telling me that
I'll suddenly forget what I
was asking and become
flustered because of your
compliment then you really
don't know me. If you two
don't want to tell me that's
fine. I'll see you guys later."
She marched off down the
hallway and then paused.
"And no, most girls don't go
around gossiping!"

Shiloh's and Evan's eyes
bugged out as they looked at
each other in panic.

"Well, now you've done it.
You really made her mad,"
Evan blamed Shiloh.

"Me! You're the one who
said she was pretty."

"Exactly. How could anyone
be mad at that?"

"Were you listening two
minutes ago?" Shiloh was
confused.

"We'll talk to her later, let's
go down to the lab."

***

Shiloh and Evan made their
way down to Evan's secret
lab. It was in the basement
of the school down a winding
staircase that no one used.

The entrance to the lab was behind a secret door that was an old bomb shelter.

When they first found this space, it had been full of old computers and equipment from decades ago. What looked like junk to Shiloh's eyes, was a treasure trove of parts and technology that Evan knew he could use for his gadgets.

Together, with the help of their friend Desirae, they cleaned up the space and it was now their headquarters for meeting up to plan projects or solve mysteries. They had recruited Roxy to join them, but she was scared of being in such an old dark lab with no windows. Even though she didn't want to hang out down there, she said she would keep the location a secret.

Once they arrived, Evan plopped the mysterious pumpkin on the table.

"I don't see anything." Shiloh studied the pumpkin.

"That's because I don't have the candle inside of it turned on. I'm going to shut off the light and turn on the candle."

"What do you mean turn on the candle?"

"It's one of those fake battery candles. I'm glad whoever left it in here didn't use a real one or the lab or maybe even the whole school could've burned down."

Evan turned on the candle
and shut off the lights.

"What is that?! This is so
creepy." Shiloh shuddered.

Where there should've been
a face carved out, was
instead a picture of some
sort of insect.

"That almost looks like...a
roach," Shiloh said with a
grimace.

"I know. It's weird. I don't know what to make of it."

"Was there anything inside of the pumpkin besides the candle?"

"Nope. This is all there was."

"Where did you find it?"

"It was right here on the table glowing. I almost peed my pants," Evan admitted.

"I gotta admit, I probably would've too."
"Let's take a look around and see if the intruder left anything by accident," Evan suggested.

Shiloh and Evan spent the next few minutes looking around the lab. It wasn't that big of a space but there were a lot of nooks and

crannies where things could
be hidden.

As they crawled on the floor
looking, they continued to
talk.

"It's weird because there's
no note or anything. I have
no idea who this person is or
what this person wants. It's
almost like, he just wants us
to know that he was here."

"How do you know it's a
guy?" Shiloh asked.

"What girl do you know, that
would carve a roach?"

"That's true for most girls,
but remember when Desirae
picked up that roach at the
beginning of the school
year?"

"Oh yeah. But still, how many of them are going to go through the trouble of carving one into a pumpkin then carry it down a dark hallway. It's pretty heavy too. I doubt a girl could lift it."

"Better not let Desirae hear that though. She's already mad at us."

They continued to look in silence until the bell rang startling them. Evan was so jumpy that he banged his head on the table he was under.

BANG

"Ow!" Evan said as he held his head. "I guess that was the first bell, we gotta go."

"Dude, you gotta relax," Shiloh tried to calm him down.

"How can I relax? I counted all my gadgets and all of them are here, but since he knows they're here, I'm scared he's going to take them or break them or something."

"I wouldn't worry about that if I were you."

"Why?" Evan asked.

"Because no one but you, knows how to work them."

"True."

Shiloh put out his hand to help Evan up.

"Wait, let me put it over there in the corner. I don't want to

walk in on this glowing thing
again." Evan turned off the
candle and put it in the
corner of the room. He made
sure to put it behind some
old computer screens so it
would be well hidden and
out of sight.

"Alright let's go," he said
when secured it.

***

"Where were you two?"
Desirae asked as soon as
she saw Evan and Shiloh in
the main hallway.

"Why do you care? I thought
you were mad at us." Shiloh
asked.

"I was, but now I'm not," she
clarified, "Evan, are you ok?"
Desirae saw him still rubbing
his head.

Shiloh rolled his eyes.
"Girls..."

"Yeah, I just hit my head,"
Evan explained, "But it might
feel better if you take a look
at it."

"Cool it, Evan. What's gotten
into you?" Desirae shook her
head.

"You're coming in too hot,"
Shiloh whispered under his
breath to Evan. He was
cringing inside, so he
decided to change the
subject. "We were in the lab.
Someone left a jack-o-
lantern with a weird
message carved in it."

"Really? I want to see it too."
She checked her watch. "Oh
man, we have to get to class
so I guess I'll wait. But at
least tell me what the

message was. And who do you think it is? Wait, how did they know about the lab? No one knows about that place."

"The only thing we can tell you that is it's a guy and he carved a picture of a roach," Evan stated.

"A roach? That's weird. But how do you know it's a guy?"

"That's what I asked him," Shiloh said, "wait till you hear his theory."

Desirae looked at him with one eyebrow up. "I'm waiting."

All of a sudden Evan thought his theory might not be so sound.

"Well?" Desirae pressed him for an explanation.

"I...uh..."

The second bell rang.

"Gotta go!" Evan ran off to his next class. "See you in there Shiloh."

"What is wrong with him today? Is it me or is there something different?"

Shiloh shrugged. He wasn't about to get in the middle of their spat.

"See you later," he said as walked towards his class.

"I'll meet you guys in the lab at lunch," Desirae called out.

Chapter 4

And Another One

At lunch Evan, Desirae and Shiloh made their way down to the lab to take a closer look at the weird message. When they got downstairs they got quite a surprise.

As soon as they opened the door they saw the pumpkin with the roach carved in it back on the table with the candle lit, but it wasn't alone. Beside it was another jack-o-lantern that had a picture of what looked like a mouse.

The lab was pitch dark except for these glowing orbs.

Shiloh and his friends were stunned into silence.

"Evan, do you see what I see?"

"Yeah, but I can't believe what I'm seeing."

"I'm guessing this is new for the both of you," Desirae stated.

"Des, I put the roach pumpkin in the corner in the back of the lab and I hid it behind some computer screens. There's no way that someone could've come and found it...unless that someone is playing a prank on me." Evan turned and gave Shiloh a pointed look.

Shiloh noticed the look and at first, he was confused, then it registered. "You think I did this?"

"You're the only one who knew where I hid the jack-o-lantern," Evan pointed out.

"I was in class right up until I saw you and Desirae to come down to the lab.

Maybe there's a hidden camera."

At this statement the trio looked around wildly to see if they were being filmed.

"Wait a minute, this is ridiculous. If there's a hidden camera it's going to be next to impossible to find. There's way too much junk in here," Desirae reasoned.

"Hey! This junk is going to help us find whoever did this. I'm going to rig my own hidden camera to catch the person." Evan started to take out random parts.

"Won't he see that you're doing that when he watches his own film?" Shiloh asked.

"That's true. I'll have to work on it when I get home and then bring it back."

"Maybe he can hear our plans too," Desirae whispered.

"YOU KNOW WHAT? I THINK IT'S A CRAZY PLAN TO MAKE MY OWN HIDDEN CAMERA! THERE'S PROBABLY NOTHING HERE!" Evan shouted, as he winked at Desirae and Shiloh exaggeratedly.

Shiloh and Desirae looked at each other and just shook their heads.

"First of all, there's no proof that there's a camera here in the first place so let's just focus on what we do know. Right in front of us is another pumpkin, this time with a mouse carved in it." Desirae pointed to the table.

They stood there and studied it for a minute. Evan got closer and traced his finger across the carving and thought out loud. "Since this is a mouse, do you think it has anything to do with the Charlie Cheese thing?"

"I don't think so. Why would they care about our lab? They're not that bad off," Shiloh answered.

"I think lunch is almost over. What are we going to do with these? We can't just take them upstairs and put them in our locker."

"Desirae's right. Since he wants us to see them so bad, why don't we just leave them here on the table," Shiloh offered.

"I agree," Evan said.

"Agreed," Desirae affirmed, "Let's get out of here."

They quietly left the pumpkins glowing on the table and ran upstairs. When they got back to the main hallway they felt safe to talk again. They stopped by Desirae's locker first.

Evan looked around before he spoke to make sure that

no one was listening. "Let's try and think what do roaches and mice have in common and let's meet here at Desirae's locker before school starts. Try and get here early so we can see if there's another pumpkin in the lab before we leave for our field trip."

Shiloh and Desirae nodded in agreement.

"What's up guys?" The group was startled by Max. They had been so focused on their plan that they didn't hear him come up.

"Nothing," Shiloh answered.

"You sure? You guys seem really serious."

"Nothing's up. We're just hanging out." Desirae tried to look relaxed.
"What's that?" Max asked.

"What's what?"

"That!" Max pointed to her shoulder.

Sitting on Desirae's right shoulder was a mouse. A fake mouse, but to Desirae it didn't matter.

"AAAAAAHHHHH!!!!"

She screamed so loud that it brought the whole hallway to a standstill.

Max burst out laughing. "Gotcha!"

"WHAT IS WRONG WITH YOU?!" Desirae was so upset. She had already been creeped out by the mystery in the lab, so she was primed to overreact to something like this.

Roxy stood closely by watching the scene trying not to laugh. Desirae immediately spotted her.

"You think this is funny too? How'd you like a rat on your shoulder or better yet, on your head?"

"Relax Desirae. It's just a prank bro, I mean sis," Max

explained, then started to laugh again. "Come on Roxy, let's go somewhere people can appreciate comedy."

"I didn't know they were good friends," Evan mused.

"Me either," Shiloh said wistfully. He had kind of liked Roxy, but he hadn't had time to get to know her better because he got caught up with the strange goings on at the school and their secret projects. Now it looked like Max beat him to it.

"Cheer up. They're probably just friends," Evan clapped him on the shoulder.

They didn't notice Desirae listening to their exchange and catch her dejected look. Evan and Shiloh knew that

Desirae had liked Shiloh, but because Evan liked Desirae, Shiloh didn't even want to go there, so he made sure he friend-zoned her. To them it was like a *Wattpad* drama.

"Hey! Do you think it's Max leaving those strange messages?" Evan asked in wonderment. "I mean, he just put a fake mouse–

"Rat," Desirae countered.

"Okay, a fake *rat* on Desirae's shoulder. He's close to Roxy and she knows about the lab. It has to be a guy because..." He looked at Desirae and decided to end his sentence before he started her up again.

"I think it could be. I'll ask Roxy if she told him," Shiloh said.

"NO! I mean, no, I'll do it." Desirae exclaimed.

They both looked at her oddly.

"If you ask her it will be too obvious. It has to come up like girl talk," she said, covering for her outburst. "I'll ask her tomorrow at the pumpkin patch."

"You're not even friends with her so how will it come up?" asked Evan.

"Don't worry about it. I'll get it out of her."

The bell rang.

"Oh boy, we really need to keep track of time. We've been late to all of our classes today!" Evan said before running off. Shiloh and Desirae took off to get to their classes too.

As they made their way to their classes, they ran right past someone who had been watching them the whole time. They had no idea that person heard their whole plan and was busy making plans of their own...

Chapter 5

Pumpkin Patch
Problems

The next morning, the three of them met up as planned. They tried not to look obvious as they snuck down to the lab. Before they opened the door, they looked at each other to prepare for what they might see.

"Ok, guys. This is the plan. I'm going to casually walk in and put my stuff down. I'm going to pretend I'm just taking stuff out of my backpack to look for something but what I'm really going to do is leave this book on the table in the corner. I removed some of the pages and I carved a tiny hole in the spine. Then I hid a small camera to record the lab."

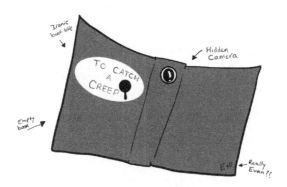

"But wouldn't he wonder why a book just happened to be lying on the table?" Shiloh asked.

"Not really, I've kind of let it get a little out of hand lately. I need to clean it up."

"True."

"Guys, we have to go to homeroom before we leave for the field trip so let's hurry up," Desirae urged.

Their palms were sweaty, Evan's breath smelled like his mom's spaghetti. Inside they were nervous, but on the outside they were relaxed and ready. They opened the door slowly, their arms were heavy. Their mouths dropped open, the words wouldn't come out. Right there on the table were not just two, but three now.

Shiloh felt like the soundtrack to his life at this moment, was one of his favorite hip hop songs.

He couldn't believe what he was seeing. A third pumpkin! This one had a mask carved in it. The mask reminded him of the type you see in Mardi Gras or in the play The Phantom of The Opera.

They all stood there and just stared. All of a sudden, Shiloh nudged Evan and looked at Evan's backpack and then back at him. This seemed to snap Evan out of it. He placed his backpack on the table and took out some books.

"Before we go to homeroom I have to make sure I brought my math book back home. After I did my homework last night I think I might've forgotten to put it back in my backpack," Evan made small talk in an attempt to look natural.

"First a roach, then a mouse, then a phantom...what's the pattern?" Desirae wondered. "I could see a roach and a mouse being related but not the phantom."

"How is a roach and a mouse related?" Shiloh asked.

"They're both gross, duh."
"That's very scientific."
Shiloh rolled his eyes.

"Guys, we have to get to homeroom now. I think I left my math book at home. Let's go by my locker so I can put away the rest of my books," Evan said.

They left calmly as if it was the most natural thing in the world to have three pumpkins with odd pictures carved in them, left by a secret intruder.

As soon as they got back upstairs they all let out a loud breath.

"I can't believe there's another one! I mean, I can believe it, because I expected it, but I can't believe it too!" Shiloh cried.

"Guys, I have a theory." Evan had his arms folded as he leaned against the lockers. He looked confident about what he was about to say.

"Well, what is it?" Desirae asked impatiently.

"Think about it. First a roach. Then what appears to be a mouse. Now a mask. Don't you see? That's not a mouse! It's a hamster."

Both Shiloh and Desirae had a look on their face that said, "so what?".

"That's your theory? That the mouse is a hamster? How can you even tell? Besides, that doesn't exactly solve anything," Shiloh stated.

"But it does! This school year has been odd. First the roaches in the sealed locker, then our hamster robot class pet, then the phantom at the spooky theater. It's all related. He's telling us that he knows we have something to do with all of it."

"But we didn't do all of those things, for example, we didn't do all the weird stuff at the theater. That was the phantom," Desirae contradicted.

"Yes, but *he* probably did. He also knows that we were investigating it."

"Evan's got a point," said Shiloh.

"I got an idea! Why don't we pick a pumpkin at the patch today and carve our own message in it and leave it on the lab table?"

"That's a great idea, Des! You always have great ideas to help us figure out things." Evan gushed.

His compliment embarrassed her but also made her smile, which she tried to hide.
"Oh boy, should I leave you two alone?" Shiloh said, annoyed by the turn of events.

"Ha. Ha. That's seriously not funny." Desirae rolled her eyes. "Here's the plan.

When we get to the pumpkin patch, I'll talk to Roxy, Evan you pick out a pumpkin and Shiloh you keep an eye on Max."

"Wait, what should I carve?" Evan asked.

"A Christmas Tree."

"Shiloh's right. Our secret project where we left presents for the children around town was the next big thing we did. We'll let him know we figured it out," Desirae said in agreement.

"I can do that easily," Evan assured the group.

"Let's hope this plan works," said Shiloh.

***

After homeroom, both classes boarded two buses and headed to the pumpkin patch. As the buses pulled in the students squealed with excitement, until they looked outside their windows. Their excitement deflated like a balloon.

This "pumpkin patch" could barely pass for one. There were rows of pumpkins ranging from small to large but that was almost all they had. There were a few stacks of hay scattered around, and a couple of mangy dogs that stood idly by waiting for the buses to come to a complete stop. Behind this scene was a corn field that looked like it needed to be watered, badly.

An old man in overalls, cowboy boots, and a straw hat, with a piece of grass in his teeth ambled over to the class as they stepped off the bus.

"Welcome to Hayworth Farms."

"Mr. Hayworth? I presume." Ms. Suffering asked, stiffly.

"Yep."

"Where is the actual farm?" She peered over her glasses and looked around.

"It's right here, missy." He extended his right arm and gestured to the sad patch of ground.

"I was told there would be a pumpkin patch."

"That's right over there."

"A maze?"

"If you go in that corn field, there's no tellin' when we'll find you. It's what we call a natural maze."

"Petting zoo?"

"You can pet the dogs, but maybe not that one over there." He motioned with his chin to a drooling dog with patches of fur missing, laying in the mud. "We don't know why she keeps eatin' rocks."

Ms. Suffering shivered.
"What about the hay rides?"

"See that there bundle of
hay? We put a saddle, and a
fake tail on it. The kids can
sit on it and pretend they're
on a pony."

"So, I take it, there's no pony
rides either."

He pointed at the hay.

"*Real* pony rides. What
about face painting?"

"My wife has that set up in the corner."

"Finally, some good news. What about food?"

"We've got water and corn."

"That's all? What about apple cider, churros, apple pie? That was in your brochure. You don't even have any pumpkin pie or pumpkin soup?"

"Ma'am, you're gonna thank me for that water when it gets around lunch time. It gets real hot in these here parts."

Ms. Suffering hadn't noticed until this time, that there was no shade.

"Is the corn boiled or maybe elote style? That would be delicious."

"You see that there field? You just go over and pick some corn and bring it home to your momma to fix." He took another look at her face. "Or in your case, your grandma."

"I've had enough! We're–

"Thank you Mr. Hayworth. I'm sure we'll have a great time." Mr. Thomas interrupted. He had been listening to the entire exchange and knew that if he didn't intervene this day was about to be even worse than it looked like it was going to be.

He half urged-half dragged
Ms. Suffering back to the
students.

"Let's be positive. Kids can
enjoy anything if they have
the right perspective," he
said, trying to encourage
her.

She looked at him and
smiled, at least what was
close to a smile. She was

actually just baring her teeth, but because she hadn't used the muscles on her face to smile in many years, she couldn't tell the difference.

Mr. Thomas didn't mind. There was a rumor at the school that they were dating, but they neither confirmed or denied it. Shiloh thought he wouldn't either if he was dating Ms. Suffering.

"Class, the pumpkin patch that was sponsored by Charlie Cheese is going to be...well...it's going to just be. Now go and pick out a pumpkin and...try not to get sick or lost," she muttered the last part softly.

"What Ms. Suffering is saying, is have fun and we'll meet you back at the bus in three hours."

"I thought we were staying the whole day?" Someone asked.

"I wouldn't do that to you guys. We're heading out in T minus 3 hours. Set your phones," he and Ms. Suffering walked off.

Shiloh, Evan, and Desirae watched the debacle unfold with the rest of the class.

"It doesn't surprise me at all that this is where Charlie Cheese paid for us to go." Shiloh shook his head.

Evan was just as disgusted but resigned to moving forward with their plan. "Let's stay focused and stick to the plan. I see Max over there. Go and keep an eye on him Shiloh. He's with Roxy, so you're going to have to find a way to get Roxy away from him for a second to talk to him Des. I'll go and pick out a pumpkin and find a corner to carve the Christmas tree in it. Ok, break!"

"This isn't a football huddle," Desirae said matter-of-factly.

"It kind of is," Evan said as he hurried off.

Desirae headed off to go and talk to Roxy. Shiloh decided that the best way to keep an eye on Max was to pretend he was doing something else close by but within range.

He decided to go and sit on the bizarre "hay-pony". "Weeeee..." he said half-heartedly as he tried to spy on Max.

He saw Desirae talking to them, but he couldn't hear what they were saying. He was so engrossed into trying to read their lips that he didn't see the dog coming towards him.

A wet tongue slapped against his cheek leaving slobber running down his face. Shiloh was so surprised by it that he fell out of the saddle and onto the ground on his back.

"Yuck! That's disgusting!" he shouted.

The dog seemed satisfied with his duty and walked back to the mud.

That was the worst part for Shiloh. It was the filthy dog that had come up to him.

None of the dogs looked friendly or cute, but that one was the worst looking out of the bunch.

He was still on his back when Max stood over him. "Looks like you made a new friend," he snickered.

So much for being inconspicuous.

"Are you going to just stand there or are you going to help me up?" Shiloh asked.

"I think I'll just stand here."

Shiloh narrowed his eyes and rolled over to get back up.

***

At the other end of the pumpkin patch, Evan was

walking through the rows closest to the corn field, trying to figure out what pumpkin would be the right size to send a message. He thought that he should choose a really big one to tell Max or whoever it was that they weren't scared, and they didn't care if they were being watched.

Unfortunately, the big ones seemed to have been rotting already and he didn't want to try and carve in mush.

Just then he felt someone tap him on his shoulder. By the time he turned around all he saw was a rustle in the field. Before he even had time to think he ran after them and into the cornfield.

As soon as he ran inside, he knew he made a mistake.

For one, it was so dry that it hurt to walk through it, second, he couldn't tell which way was back towards the patch versus which way drew him deeper in. He had no idea how large the cornfield was.

He thought he heard some rustling to his left and ran towards it. But he had to stop because he didn't hear anything anymore. He stood stock still waiting to see if he heard anything. A small rustle sound was now to his right, which made him to run off in that direction now. But as before, he had to stop because he didn't hear anything.

"Okay! I give up! I know it's you, Max! You can show yourself now! The jig is up!"

Nothing. Not a sound.

"MAX!" Evan shouted.

"Max?" He said again
weakly.

All of a sudden there was a
loud whoop from behind that
startled Evan and made him
trip over his feet, causing
him to fall forward on his
face. Dazed, Evan slowly got
up to see...a pumpkin...with
a Christmas tree carved in it.

***

Desirae who had finally
convinced Roxy to come
with her to find the bathroom
so she could help her fix her
hair, was trying to come up
with a way to bring up the
lab. As they made their way
across the dusty pumpkin
patch she struggled to find a
neutral topic.

"So, you and Max huh?"

"Me and Max what?" Roxy answered suspiciously.

"Are you two boyfriend and girlfriend?"

"What? No! We're friends. I'm too young for that. Besides, I like...well, that's not important."

"Then why are you two hanging out so much?"

"Because that's what friends do. I don't ask you why you're around Shiloh and Evan every second of the day."

Desirae blushed at that. "I'm...uh...we're friends..."

"Exactly. It's not like you guys let anyone else into your little club, so why wouldn't I hang around someone who does."

"It's not a club!" Desirae defended herself.

"I thought for a second we were going to be good friends, but then you guys left me out of your secret projects just because I didn't want to hang out in that dingy lab."

They stopped walking. "That dingy lab happens to be my best friend's lab where he makes all sorts of awesome gadgets, so you better watch what you say."

"Or what?"

"Or...I'll tell Shiloh that you told Max about the secret lab."

"That's not true! I didn't tell anyone about it. You shouldn't threaten someone with lies."

"Well, if you didn't tell Max, then how does he know about it?"

"What makes you think Max knows anything about it?"

"Someone's leaving us strange messages and we figured it was either you or him, but we figured it was him because you don't like going down there."

"Well, it's not as if the lab is that much of a secret. It is in a school not some abandoned cave."

"Yeah, but no one goes down there."

"I guess someone does. I don't think it's Max though, and I can't ask him, or he'll wonder why I didn't tell him about the lab to begin with."

"What makes you think he has nothing to do with it?" Desirae asked.

"We have better things to do than spy on you guys. I'm going to pick out a pumpkin now. As for your hair, maybe, bring a brush next time and hit the kitchen in the back." Roxy walked off.

Desirae patted the back of her hair and was now determined to find a mirror to see what Roxy was talking about.

***

Desirae and Shiloh met up
first by the buses.

"Shiloh, why do you have dirt
all over you?"

"Because one of those dogs
licked me on my face and
made me fall out of the
saddle."

"I thought there weren't any
pony rides."

"There's not. I just went on
the hay-pony to try and spy
on Max."

"Are you sure you just didn't
want to pretend that you
were on a pony?" Desirae
giggled.

"Real funny. I didn't even get to spy on Max because when I fell out of the saddle I guess I made a huge scene and he came over and laughed at me the rest of the day."

"My talk didn't go so well either. I did get the info we needed, but it's got me wondering. Do you think we're a clique?"

"No, who said that? Isn't a clique a girl thing?"

Desirae rolled her eyes. "What is with you and Evan lately? Do you think we're a club then? Like an exclusive club?"

"No...well actually, we do have a secret lab which is kind of like a clubhouse and we plan stuff that no one knows about so maybe we are. Why?"

"Roxy made it seem like we're an exclusive club that we keep her and Max out of."

"But we told her about the lab!"

"Yeah, but she said that just because she didn't like to hang out in the din-, I mean club, she shouldn't have been left out of our group."

"She has a point."

Evan walked up slowly lugging two pumpkins. "How did the plan go for you guys? I'm beat." Evan plopped on the ground, exhausted.

"What's wrong with you?
Why are you so tired?"
Desirae asked concerned.

"I got lost in the cornfield."

"The cornfield! It looks so
scary there with all the dried
stocks and crows feeding on
the rotten corn."

"Well, someone tapped me
on the shoulder and then ran
into the field. I chased them
and ended up getting lost.
But I eventually used the
sun's direction as a compass
and found my way out of
there."

"Wow, imagine if you weren't
some scientist and you went
in there. You'd just have to
move in there and call it
home," Shiloh said.

"Why do you have two pumpkins?" asked Desirae.

"One is for our pumpkin flavored project, and the other was a gift."

"A gift?"

"From our mysterious messenger." Evan turned the pumpkin around to reveal the pumpkin with the Christmas Tree carved in it.

"What! Where did he give it to you? That means you saw who it was then, right?" Desirae asked excitedly.

"Well, not exactly. I was on the floor on my face and I looked up and the pumpkin was right in front of me. He left it there and ran before I could see who it was."

"Why were you on your face?" Shiloh asked.

"He pushed me from behind."

"He pushed you? This is getting serious," Desirae said worriedly.

"Well, not exactly pushed. He startled me and I...accidentally tripped..." He said embarrassed.

"Oh," she responded to this bit of information as neutrally as possible.

She looked at Shiloh and they couldn't help it. They both burst out laughing.

"Oh that's good. Laugh it up guys. When you're done, maybe we can get back to finding out who it was."

"Well, Max was with me for at least a part of the day, so I'm not sure if it was him" said Shiloh.

"I don't think it's him either because Roxy says she didn't tell a soul about the lab."

"Do you believe her?" Evan asked.

"I do. She looked offended that I would even question her and she said that her and Max had better things to do then to spy on us."

They were quiet at that last statement because they didn't seem to have anything better to do than to spy on Max and Roxy. It was awkward.

The silence of the three of them was broken by someone wailing. They looked up to see Ms. Suffering waving at everyone to get back to the bus.

"Class! We are leaving! Stop crying Britney! It's not that noticeable." Ms. Suffering patted a classmate of theirs who was bawling her eyes out.

The thing that shocked them was that her whole face was bright orange with black circles around her eyes.

"It won't come off!" She cried.

"I'm going to sue you Mr. Hayworth! Mrs. Hayworth, you should be ashamed of yourself for using permanent marker instead of face paint!"

Mr. Hayworth quickly walked over. "We didn't mean no harm. Face paint's expensive. We thought the markers would do just fine. We didn't know it wouldn't come off."

"What part of permanent do you not understand?" Ms. Suffering asked, annoyed. She didn't even wait for an answer. "Students get back in the bus!"

Shiloh and his friends could see that there were quite a few people who were in tears. Their faces were all marked up with different colors and designs. He thought he wouldn't want to be Ms. Suffering or Mr. Thomas when the parents

saw their kids faces and
realized that it would be
weeks, maybe even months
before it would fade.

"I'm so glad I was in the
cornfield. I'd rather be lost
over there than get my face
"painted" with permanent
marker." Evan made air
quotes with the word
painted.

"But why did they let Mrs.
Hayworth do that?"

"Maybe they were told that it
was a special face paint that

would last longer. A *lot* longer."

They started laughing.

Ms. Suffering zeroed in on the trio. She didn't have to say a word. They stopped laughing immediately and got on the bus.

Chapter 6

The Watcher

The next morning Shiloh was running late again. He had a hard time waking up for school because had stayed up all night planning the revenge prank on his sister Shasha. It required a lot of work, but it would be worth it.

By the time he got to school, the hallway was empty with everyone in their homeroom classes.

Oh, no. Shiloh thought I don't want to walk in late. *Please let there be a sub instead of Ms. Sufferin. Please let her miss school just once, and let that once be today.*

As soon as he opened the
door heard a shrill, "Shiloh!".
Ms. Sufferin never missed
school. She was rudely
healthy despite her sour
attitude.

"Nice of you to join us. I think
you may be confused as to
what the morning bell
means. It isn't a suggestion
of when to start. It is actually
the time when school starts.
No later! Is that clear?"

"Yes, ma'am."

Shiloh had been distracted
by the scolding by Ms.
Suffering that he didn't
notice half of the class with
marker still on their faces.
He tried not to laugh, but he
couldn't help smiling.

"Is there something funny
young man?"

"No..."

"Do you find it funny that half of your class looks like they belong in the circus?"

"Umm....no..."

"Good! I spent my night ignoring angry calls and sending apology emails to their parents. My whole night was ruined. I had to miss my favorite show, Watching Paint Dry, but I was still able to watch the spinoff, Watching Water Boil."

"What? Those are actual shows?" Shiloh asked before he caught himself. He wondered why he did this over and over. Why did he provoke her?

"What do you mean? Those are fascinating shows. I bet you don't know which color paint dries the fastest or what type of water boils faster." She turned to address the class. "Nothing better happen today people. My new show, which is the spin off, of the spin off,

comes on tonight. It's called
Watching Grass Grow."

Shiloh thought Ms. Suffering
couldn't get any weirder, but
she did. She always did.

"Ok class, tomorrow is our
contest, so I hope you've
been planning out your
pumpkin dish. Charlie
Cheese will be here to gift us
our new lab computer and
present the prizes. Make
sure you bring them warm
and ready. Come with an
empty stomach. It will be the
first thing we do for the day.
It might be the only thing we
do if the dishes are as
disgusting as I think they'll
be," she muttered. "Any
questions?"

A few people asked
questions about what they
were allowed to bring but

Shiloh didn't hear it. He was looking at his texts.

Evan to Shiloh:

Did Desirae tell you yet?

Shiloh to Evan:

Tell me what?

Evan to Shiloh:

We found another one. Guess what it had in the middle?

Shiloh to Evan:

I can't guess right now. I can barely read these texts without risking getting into trouble.

Evan to Shiloh:

A broken heart.

Shiloh to Evan:

Are you sure this is a guy?

Evan to Shiloh:

I'm starting to wonder too.

Shiloh to Evan:

Did you take a look at the tape?

Evan to Shiloh:

I did, but there was nothing conclusive. I think they knew they were going to be recorded because they came in with baggy clothes, hoodie, and gloves. There was no way to make out who they were. The first thing they did when they came in was to reach in and turn the camera off.

Shiloh to Evan:

So, it really could be a girl. With the way Desirae described how upset Roxy was, maybe she's the one who's been doing it all along and not Max.

Evan to Shiloh:

I think we need to invite her down the lab and show her how much nicer it is since the first day she saw it. Then we can interrogate her.

Shiloh to Evan:

I hope you're joking.

Evan to Shiloh:

LOL. I was just seeing what you were going to say. I know you have a crush on her.

Shiloh to Evan:

No I don't.

Evan to Shiloh:

Are you still stuck on Gabrielle?

Gabrielle was a girl in his sister's class that Shiloh had a crush on several months ago, but because he hadn't seen her around in a long time, the feeling had faded. She was beautiful and exotic to Shiloh because she was French. But what made her unique and interesting also became a barrier for him to get to know her. They had a lot of differences, and it was hard to talk to her because he couldn't understand her accent.

At least, that's what Shiloh told himself. The truth was that she started to date someone in her class and Shiloh was friend-zoned.

Shiloh to Evan:

I'm not stuck on anyone.

Evan to Shiloh:

Anyways, since you have science with Max and Roxy, you should invite both of them.

Shiloh to Evan:

Both of them? Why? Max is...

Evan to Shiloh:

It's better to keep your friends close and your enemies even closer.

Shiloh didn't agree with him, at least when it came to Max, but it was Evan's lab and he would do as he asked.

***

Later, in Mrs. Engelstrom's science class Shiloh decided to talk to Max and Roxy before it started. He purposely sat in the row right next to them. Max was seated in front of Roxy towards the back of the room. Shiloh observed them for a bit before he spoke.

He noticed that Max and Roxy really looked like they were friends, but if he wasn't mistaken it also looked like Max might have caught feelings for her. It was in the way he seemed to try and impress her with his jokes and the way that he looked at her even when she didn't know. It didn't look like Roxy knew, or if she did, she didn't' acknowledge it.

"Hey guys." Shiloh said.

"Hey Shiloh. Is your back sore?" Max asked in a mocking tone.

"No, but thanks for nothing."

"What are you two talking about?" Roxy asked.

"Nothing." Shiloh quickly changed the subject. "So, I wanted to talk to you two about something."

"If it's what Desirae talked to me about, then I really don't want to talk."

"Roxy, hear me out. We were talking, and we think that you guys should come down to our secret lab at lunch."

"Your secret what?" Max looked confused and amused.

Shiloh cringed. He didn't know why Evan insisted on inviting both of them.

"Lab. Evan has a secret lab, here at the school, but you have to promise you won't tell anyone where it is. You have to pretend that you don't even know it exists. Roxy's seen it and she said she never told you about it, which may have been the truth."

"May have been the truth? I don't lie."

"You didn't tell me?" Max looked hurt at first, but then he saw Shiloh watching him and cleared his throat. "I mean, cool, you didn't tell me."

Shiloh was cringing again, but this time at Max.

"Well, this is awkward," Shiloh stated.

"Sorry, but I promised I wouldn't say anything. I'm good at keeping secrets. Besides, if you told me something, which you have, you wouldn't want me to tell Shiloh would you?"

For some reason it bothered Shiloh that they had their own secrets. He didn't know why it bothered him since he and Evan and Desirae had a ton of secrets. He figured it felt different when you weren't being the one left out. He thought to himself that this is probably what Roxy, and maybe even Max, felt about him and his friends.

"What do you guys do there?" asked Max.

"I'll explain at lunch. If you're in, meet us at Evan's locker."

"Ok class! Let's start!" Mrs. Engelstrom clapped her hands together to get everyone's attention.

***

The lunch bell rang signaling they had a break for a good forty minutes. Evan, Shiloh, and Desirae stood in front of

Evan's locker waiting for
Roxy and Max.

Five minutes passed and still
no sign of them.

"We need every minute we
can get. If they don't show
up in the next five minutes
lets go down without them,"
Shiloh said. He secretly
hoped they wouldn't show
up, at least not Max.

"There. I see them." Desirae
nodded in the direction that
they were coming from.

"Took you guys long enough," Shiloh complained.

"I had to do some convincing," Roxy said.

"Well, you don't have to come Max. We'll understand."

"I'm here, aren't I? Let's go to this secret lab," Max said loudly.

"Shhh!" The rest of them hushed him.

"See, this is what I'm talking about." Shiloh turned to Evan smugly.

"Max, before we take you down there, do you promise not to say a word?"

"You guys take this stuff too seriously." Max rolled his eyes.

"Please Max," Roxy asked. She put her hand on his arm softly.

"Ok, ok. I promise," He said to Evan. He turned to Roxy. "Are you happy?" Although he said it sarcastically Shiloh could see he really was asking her.

"Thank you." Roxy said.

The five them made their way down the hallway. When the coast was clear they quietly went behind the hidden door and down the winding staircase.

Evan opened the door and brought them inside. Max was uncharacteristically quiet on the way there and he was still silent as he looked around.

"Wow Evan, this place looks so much better!" Roxy exclaimed. "Not that it didn't look good before...actually it didn't look good at all, but you saw the potential and now it looks like a real lab." She put her hand on his shoulder.

Evan looked self-conscious with having her hand on his shoulder. He saw Max, Shiloh, and Desirae with stormy looks on their faces and decided he better shift a little and move away from Roxy or there might be trouble.

Evan knew Max was probably mad because he clearly liked Roxy. He thought Shiloh had a crush on her too, maybe not as big as Max's but it was still there. What he couldn't figure out was Desirae. He knew Desirae knew that he had a crush on her, but she seemed to like Shiloh sometimes, and sometimes it looked like she kind of liked Evan. When they went to the dance a few months ago, she danced most of the dances with him and it made him so happy. But since then, it was like she friend-zoned him and started to focus on Shiloh again. He couldn't figure her out.

But now, she looked like she was about snap at Roxy if she didn't move her hand. She was jealous! It made Evan warm inside and he couldn't stop smiling.

Unfortunately, Desirae misread his smiling and thought it was because of Roxy. "Let's keep our hands to ourselves ok. When we're down here it's to hang out *as friends* and plan projects," Desirae said pointedly.

Uh, oh. Evan thought. She really did snap.

"Sorry. I didn't mean anything by that..."Roxy said worriedly. She wanted to be better friends with all of them, especially Shiloh, and she knew that the key was to be closer to Desirae. This wasn't going as she had planned.

"What do you think Max?" Evan asked him.

"I think that...this is nerd city."

"Max!" Roxy gasped.

"I mean that in a good way. Being a nerd and into tech and gadgets is cool now," Max explained. "But what's with all of these pumpkins? I think you guys might be spending too much time down here. You're supposed to carve a face in the pumpkins not weird symbols."

"That's why we invited you down here. We wanted to ask you, actually both of you, point blank. Are you guys leaving these down here?" Shiloh asked. He had enough of the small talk.

"What? Why would I do that? You think I would take the time to carve out a weird picture and sneak down here? I've never seen this room before."

"That's what I told them Max." Roxy turned to Shiloh. "Is that the only reason you invited us?"

"No, Desirae told us what you said about leaving you guys out, so we wanted to invite you to hang out as well as ask you if you had anything to do with this."

"Well, now that you know it's not us. Who are your other suspects?" Roxy asked.

"We don't have any other ones..." Desirae said sheepishly.

"You mean you guys hung your whole case on us?" Roxy was shocked.

"No...well maybe." Shiloh looked equally just as awkward.

"Ok, let's think. Who else could be doing this?" Evan asked the group.

"Well, tell us what you guys think the symbols mean first," Max said.

Evan explained how each of the symbols had something to do with a project or investigation they all were involved in. They reasoned that the person who was responsible for this was letting them know that they were watching them.

"So The Watcher wants to send you a message. There has to be more than just saying he's watching you. Do you think he wants you to stop? Do you think he just wants to scare you? What else do you think he wants?" Roxy asked.

"I've been thinking about it," Evan said, "And I think if he wanted us to stop he would've done more than leave these pumpkins. I think he wants us to not only know he's watching us, but when the time is right he might ask for something. I think it's his way to try and control us by letting us know that he sees everything."

"Whoa! Should we tell someone?" Desirae asked.

"No, not unless it turns serious. For now, I think we're safe. We'll just wait for the next message," Evan instructed. "Do you guys agree?"

The rest of them nodded in agreement.

"Lunch is almost over, let's get out of here. Before you guys leave, do you want to name our group something cool like Cornerstone Detectives or Cornerstone P.I.?"

"That is so lame Evan," Shiloh said and laughed.

"What? I thought it was cool," Evan defended himself.

"I thought you said this wasn't a club Desirae," Roxy said.

"It's not. But Evan's on the right track. We need a code name to use when we set up a meeting."

"But what if we just want to hang out?" Shiloh asked.

"Then we don't need one for that. The code name should only be used when it has to do with The Watcher," Evan said.

"I vote for Pentagon because it has five sides, and we're five people," Max said, surprising the group with his willingness to participate.

"Everyone agree?" Evan asked.

Once again, they all nodded in agreement.

"Ok, Let's go," Desirae said.

Chapter 7

ICU

The time had finally come for the Charlie Cheese Pumpkin Flavor Contest. All morning students had been arriving with their dishes smelling of various pumpkin flavors. The scent was so strong in the cafeteria that Ms. Sufferin complained she was getting a migraine. She ran around and flung open the windows.

Rows of dishes lined the tables, from normal pumpkin pie, pumpkin muffins, and pumpkin cookies to creative recipes like pumpkin lasagna, pumpkin flavored chicken, pumpkin sushi, and pumpkin dumplings. Then there were the just plain bizarre ones like pumpkin slushies, pumpkin lollipops, pumpkin soda, and spaghetti with pumpkin sauce.

Ms. Sufferin was turning green just looking at the horrifying food. She didn't know how anyone could win this contest. Even the normal food looked gross because she just felt that there shouldn't be anything flavored with pumpkin besides a plain old pumpkin, and that should only be eaten by rabbits and other animals. She hated pumpkins!

The Charlie Cheese mouse mascot and his coworkers were waiting in the corner scrolling on their phones waiting for the contest to start. Everything was in place. The new computer that they were donating had been set up on the table and had a red ribbon around it. The food was all organized anonymously with the numbers attached to each dish, so everyone could vote and not just choose their friends. Ms. Suffering reasoned that everyone probably knew what their friends brought anyway but it at least needed to look fair.

Ms. Suffering and Mr. Thomas went to the front of the cafeteria.

Mr. Thomas started the announcement. "Ok class,

now is when the taste test begins. We're going to take a small portion of each dish and write down the number of the food you like the best. After we've had our fill we'll tally up the votes. Do you have anything to add Agony, I mean Ms. Sufferin."

Agony?! That was Ms. Sufferin's first name? Shiloh thought the name was totally fitting but the worst name a parent could ever name a child.

She looked at the students. "If anyone of you ever call me by my first name you'll find the true meaning of what agony truly is. Besides that, I have nothing to add. Let's get this over with." She quickly looked at her sponsors who were still scrolling. "I mean let's eat!"

The class went dish by dish in order of the numbers. Everyone had made their dishes ready to be tasted. They were either in pieces, small cups, or on toothpicks.

"Evan what did you bring?" Shiloh whispered.

"I made Pumpkin edible slime."
"That is so gross. Slime is bad already, to make it edible is disgusting, to top it off by making it pumpkin flavored is the worst thing imaginable. I feel like vomit might taste better, or at least be close to it."

"Thanks for your vote of confidence Shiloh. You might be surprised by how much you like it. You gotta try it or I'll tell Ms. Sufferin,"

Evan teased. "What did you bring?"

"I brought pumpkin juice."

"What!? And you think mine is bad?"

"People juice vegetables all the time, like beets, celery, spinach, kale."

"Yeah, but never pumpkin! Did you at least add anything to make it taste better like cinnamon or sugar or something? Anything?"

"Nope. I'm going to get extra points because it's going to be healthy. I even left the pulp."

"I just threw up in my mouth," Evan gagged.

They continued to taste the dishes and overall it was as bad as everyone thought it was going to be. Several people started to feel sick and had to go sit down. Only people with iron stomachs could make it through the whole contest.

By the end of it, Ms. Sufferin could barely stand to announce the winner. She was clammy and complained of mild stomach cramps. Mr. Thomas was no better.

"You kids are horrible. Just horrible. To put us through that was unconscionable. The food was terrible, an absolute abomination. Why couldn't at least the muffins or the pie be good? Do any of you have any home training for cooking? Is this what you fix yourselves? No wonder you're all so skinny."

Mr. Thomas cleared his throat to interrupt her rant. "Just announce the winners so I can go to the bathroom," he whispered.

"Third place goes to the pumpkin muffins, although I'm still not sure what the crunchy black things were."

A girl from Mr. Thomas's homeroom started clapping excitedly.

"Second place goes to the pumpkin sushi." Another girl jumped up happily.

"I just want to say, that next time, you should cook the rice another maybe twenty minutes."

"Cook? I thought sushi was supposed to be raw," the girl answered.

"You mean that rice was raw?" Ms. Sufferin just shook her head.

"And now for the grand prize. Let's see." She opened up the envelope. "The winner is number 12. Number 12 was...you gotta be kidding me. That was the edible slime."

"YES!!!" Evan cheered. He ran up to the front and posed with and got his new phone and posed with the mascot. After the photo, the workers and mascot went back to scrolling.

"We did it. It's over. Class dismissed. In fact, if you need to go to the nurse's station go ahead. The rest of you, go to the library until school's out. I need to go home." Ms. Sufferin walked off stage and out of the cafeteria. Mr. Thomas went the other way holding his butt as he ran to the bathroom.

Desirae, Roxy, and Max came up to Evan and Shiloh.

"Are you guys sick too?" Desirae asked the group.

"I'm a bit queasy," Roxy answered.

"I'm good," Max said.

"Me too." Both Shiloh and Evan said.

None of them looked good, but they weren't about to admit that to the girls.

"I'm just going to get something from the lab before I head over the library. I'll meet you guys there."

Ten minutes later a text went to the group chat:

Code Pentagon

The group snuck out of the library one by one and headed down to the lab.

"What's going on?" Shiloh asked Evan as soon as he walked in.

"This. This is what's going on." He pointed to another pumpkin, but this time the letter I-C-U were carved and under it was an image of two eyes.

"What does this mean?" Desirae asked.

"I think ICU and the two eyes means he sees us and is watching us. Maybe we'll get more clues in order to figure out who it is and what he wants. Until we know more, don't say a word.

***

Later that night, Shiloh was finally going to put his plan into place. All week he had been working on it and tonight was the night. This revenge prank was going to be sweet. It was midnight, and everyone was fast asleep, including Shasha.

The house was pitch black especially in Shasha's room. She didn't sleep with any nightlights on or with the bathroom light on. She liked it completely dark.

"Oh Shaaashaaa!" Shiloh called out in a sing-song voice.

Shasha fidgeted a bit in her sleep.

"Shaaashaaa!" Shiloh called out a bit louder.

"What Shiloh? I'm sleeping."

"Shasha!" Shiloh yelled out.

Shasha turned quickly to yell at Shiloh and was greeted by dozens of creepy looking jack-o-lanterns with ghoulish faces staring back at her.

"AAAAAAAHHHHH!!!!"

Her scream woke everyone up, maybe even the neighborhood. He could hear his parents murmuring in their room.

"And that's how you get back big sisters! Good night folks." Shiloh said to the phone.

"Shiloh! You recorded that! My hair is in a scarf! Everyone's going to see my pj's? I'm going to get you

back Shiloh!" Shasha yelled
as Shiloh left the room.

All she heard was his faint
laughing down the hall.

Epilogue

That same night, while everyone was tucked safely in their beds, sound asleep, except for maybe Shasha, there was someone else who was up planning.

"They think they have me figured out. They think they know what my next move is. Little do they know what's coming. I've got plans. I saw how they worked together to solve the mystery of the sealed locker, and how they almost got exposed with that class pet fraud. But they didn't know what to do about the strange occurrences at the Leroux theater. I almost had the class in my grip, but those nosy kids stopped me. The last straw was that Secret Santa campaign when they brought presents to all the needy kids in town. Who did they think they were? There's only one Santa, duh. I wouldn't even have had to make myself known to them if they had stayed distracted with their little love triangles and secret admirers. It was time to enact plan B."

"They want to know who I am. Maybe I'll let them know, someday. For now, I think I'll keep them busy. They won't even know that I'll be keeping them busy to keep them away from my real plan..."

A soft eerie laugh escaped The Watcher's lips as they turned off the light and went to sleep dreaming of their devious plans.

The nightlight came on immediately. It shined just bright enough to show a huge shadow on the ceiling. The shadow of two huge eyes...

Acknowledgments

I want to thank my family again for their support. Your continual affirmation and encouragement are what keep me going. I love you and thank you.

About the Author

Rita Onyx is a member of the Onyx Family who also include Mirthell, Shalom, Sinead, Shasha, and Shiloh. Together they have a successful social media and YouTube following with over 4 million subscribers and over 1 billion views across their channels. You can find them on Onyx Flix and YouTube. You can also hear Rita Onyx along with the family on The Onyx Life Podcast.

Other Onyx Kids Books:

Onyx Kids School Days:
The Sealed Locker
The Class Pet Fraud
The Phantom of the School Play
The Secret Santa
The Secret Admirer
The Spooky Cipher

Onyx Kids Adventures:
Pop Me If You Dare
Zombie Outbreak
Kidnapped by a Dragon
Headless Horseman
Don't Leave the Door Open
'Twas The Fright Before Christmas
Welcome To The Prey Ground

Getting to Know Onyx Kids